WITHDRAWN

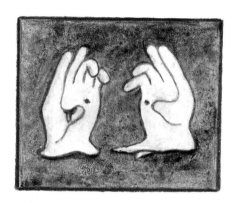

to my grandmother, ida waye

first published in 2009 by simply read books
www.simplyreadbooks.com

text & illustrations copyright © 2009 lynn e. ray

library and archives canada cataloguing in publication

ray, lynn
     hallelujah / lynn e. ray.

isbn 978-1-897476-07-9

    1. stories without words. i. title.

nc143.r39a68 2009   c813'.6   c2009-904064-6

we gratefully acknowledge for
their financial support of our
publishing program the canada
council for the arts, the bc arts
council, and the government of
canada through the book publishing industry development
program (bpidp).

this book is typeset in democratica
book design by jumin lee

10 9 8 7 6 5 4 3 2 1

printed in singapore

hallelujah

Lynn E. Ray

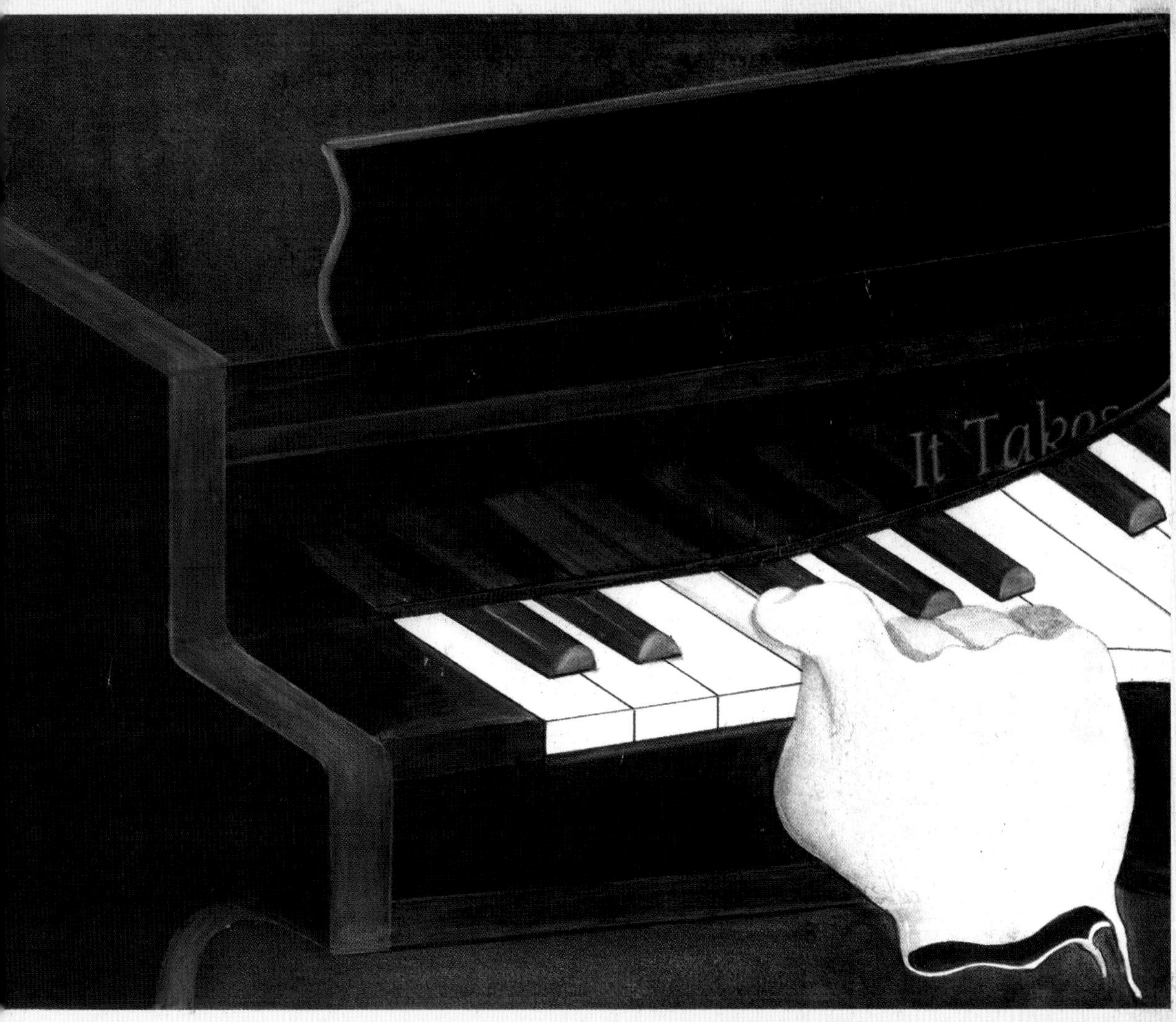

"we love because he first loved us."

1 john 4:19